For Buchi Emecheta M.H.
For Joe C.B.

ISBN 0-590-46009-9

Text copyright © 1991 by Mary Hoffman.
Illustrations copyright © 1991 by Caroline Binch.
All rights reserved. Published by Scholastic Inc.,
730 Broadway, New York, NY 10003, by arrangement
with Dial Books for Young Readers, a Division of
Penguin Books USA Inc. Published in Great Britain by
Frances Lincoln Limited.

12   7 8/9

Printed in the U.S.A.   09

First Scholastic printing, September 1993

Amazing Grace

by **Mary Hoffman**
pictures by **Caroline Binch**

SCHOLASTIC INC.
New York   Toronto   London   Auckland   Sydney

Grace was a girl who loved stories.

She didn't mind if they were read to her or told to her or made up in her own head. She didn't care if they were in books or movies or out of Nana's long memory. Grace just loved stories.

After she had heard them, and sometimes while they were still going on, Grace would act them out. And she always gave herself the most exciting part.

Grace went into battle as Joan of Arc . . .

and wove a wicked web as Anansi the Spider.

She hid inside the wooden horse at the gates of Troy. . . .

She went exploring for lost kingdoms. . . .

She sailed the seven seas
with a peg leg
and a parrot.

She was Hiawatha, sitting by the shining Big-Sea-Water. . .

and Mowgli in the backyard jungle.

Most of all Grace loved to act out adventure stories and fairy tales. When there was no one else around, Grace played all the parts herself.

She set out to seek her fortune, with no companion but her trusty cat—and found a city with streets paved in gold.

Or she was Aladdin, rubbing his magic lamp to make the genie appear.

Sometimes she could get Ma and Nana to join in,
when they weren't too busy.

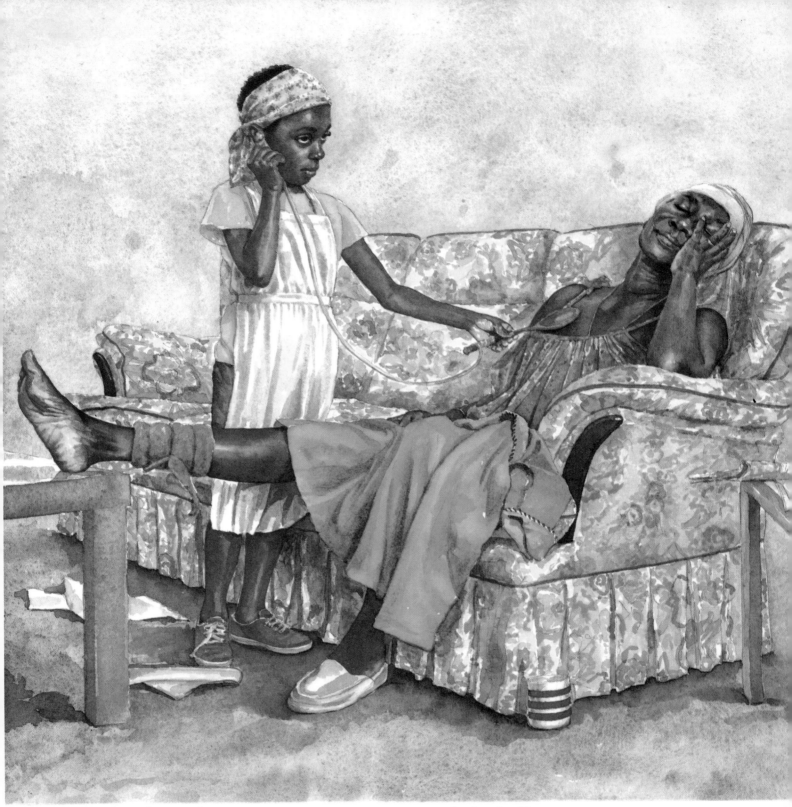

Then she was Doctor Grace and their lives were
in her hands.

One day Grace's teacher said they would do the
play *Peter Pan*. Grace knew who she wanted to be.
When she raised her hand, Raj said, "You can't
be Peter—that's a boy's name."
But Grace kept her hand up.

"You can't be Peter Pan," whispered Natalie.
"He isn't black." But Grace kept her hand up.
"All right," said the teacher. "Lots of you want
to be Peter Pan, so we'll have auditions next week to
choose parts." She gave them words to learn.

When Grace got home,
she seemed sad.

"What's the matter?"
asked Ma.

"Raj said I can't be
Peter Pan because I'm a girl."

"That just shows what Raj
knows," said Ma. "A girl
can be Peter Pan if she
wants to."

Grace cheered up, then later she remembered
something else. "Natalie says I can't be Peter Pan
because I'm black," she said.

Ma looked angry. But before she could speak,
Nana said, "It seems that Natalie is another one who
don't know nothing. You can be anything you want,
Grace, if you put your mind to it."

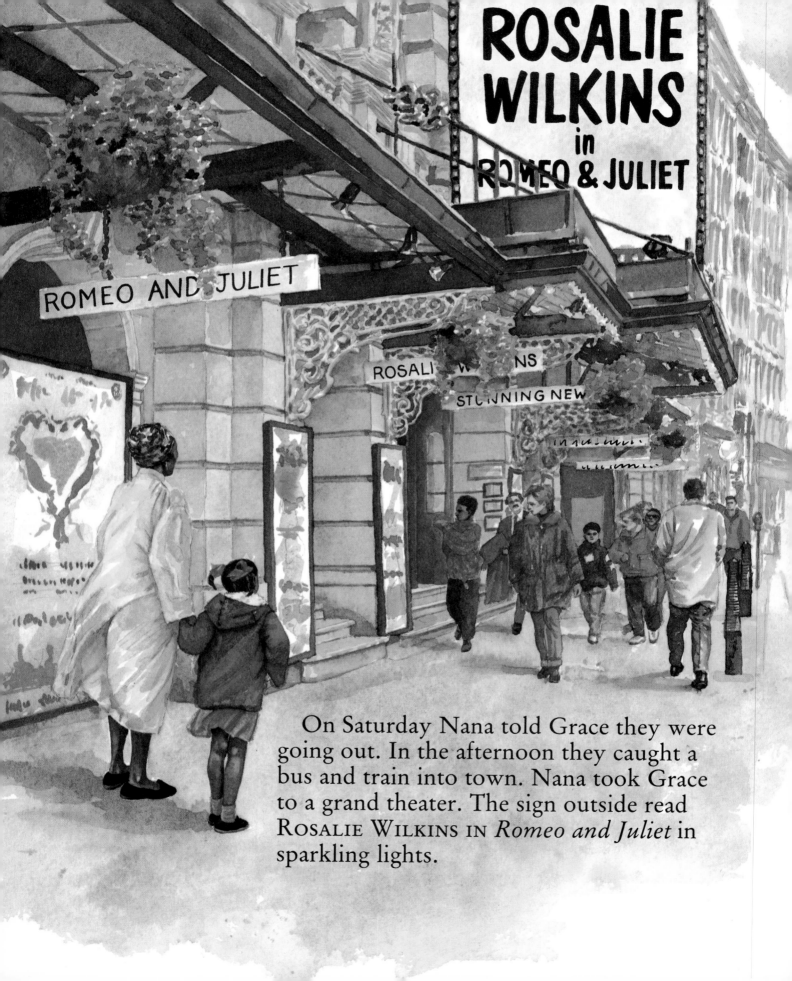

On Saturday Nana told Grace they were going out. In the afternoon they caught a bus and train into town. Nana took Grace to a grand theater. The sign outside read ROSALIE WILKINS IN *Romeo and Juliet* in sparkling lights.

"Are we going to the ballet, Nana?" asked Grace.

"We are, honey, but first I want you to look at this picture."

Grace looked up and saw a beautiful young ballerina in a tutu. Above the dancer it said STUNNING NEW JULIET.

"That one is little Rosalie from back home in Trinidad," said Nana. "Her granny and me, we grew up together on the island. She's always asking me do I want tickets to see her Rosalie dance—so this time I said yes."

After the ballet Grace played the part of Juliet,
dancing around her room in her imaginary tutu.
I can be anything I want, she thought.

On Monday the class met for auditions to choose who was best for each part.

When it was Grace's turn to be Peter, she knew exactly what to do and all the words to say—she had been Peter Pan all weekend. She took a deep breath and imagined herself flying.

When it was time to vote, the class chose Raj to be Captain Hook and Natalie to be Wendy. There was no doubt who would be Peter Pan. *Everyone* voted for Grace.

"You were fantastic!" whispered Natalie.

The play was a big success and Grace was an
amazing Peter Pan.

After it was all over, she said, "I feel as if I could
fly all the way home!"

"You probably could," said Ma.

"Yes," said Nana. "If Grace put her mind to it,
she can do anything she want."